For Emelia, with love
– D.H.

For Anthony, Jane, Mark,
Katy and Alice, with love
– J.C.

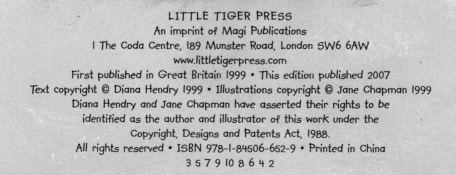

LITTLE TIGER PRESS
An imprint of Magi Publications
1 The Coda Centre, 189 Munster Road, London SW6 6AW
www.littletigerpress.com
First published in Great Britain 1999 • This edition published 2007
Text copyright © Diana Hendry 1999 • Illustrations copyright © Jane Chapman 1999
Diana Hendry and Jane Chapman have asserted their rights to be
identified as the author and illustrator of this work under the
Copyright, Designs and Patents Act, 1988.
All rights reserved • ISBN 978-1-84506-652-9 • Printed in China
3 5 7 9 10 8 6 4 2

The Very Noisy Night

Diana Hendry   Jane Chapman

LITTLE TIGER PRESS
London

It was the middle of the night, and Big Mouse was fast asleep in his big bed. Little Mouse was wide awake in his little bed. "Big Mouse! Big Mouse!" called Little Mouse. "I can hear something rushing round the house, huffing and puffing."

Big Mouse opened one eye and one ear.
"It's only the wind," he said.

"Can I come into your bed?" asked Little Mouse.
"No," said Big Mouse. "There isn't room."
And he turned over and went back to sleep.

Little Mouse lay listening to the wind. Then, suddenly, between a huff and a puff, came a . . .

TAP TAP TAP

TAP

Little Mouse climbed out of bed, opened the front door — just a crack — and peeped out.

WHOOOSH!

went the wind, but there was no one oulside. "Big Mouse! Big Mouse!" called Little Mouse. "I can hear someone tapping. Perhaps there's a burglar on the roof."

Big Mouse got out of
bed and opened the bedroom
curtains. "Look," he said, "it's
only a branch tapping on the
window. Go back to sleep."
"Can I come into your bed?"
asked Little Mouse.
"No," said Big Mouse.
"You wriggle."

Little Mouse lay in his own bed and listened to the wind huffing and puffing and the branch tap-tapping — and someone calling,

"HOO-HOO! HOO-HOO!"

Little Mouse climbed out of bed again. This time he looked under it. Then he looked in the wardrobe, and feeling very frightened he cried, "Big Mouse! Big Mouse! I think there's a ghost in the house, and it's looking for me. It keeps calling, who who? who who?"

Big Mouse sighed, sat up
and listened. "It's only an owl,"
he said. "It's awake, like you."
"Can I come into your bed?"
asked Little Mouse.
"No," said Big Mouse. "Your
paws are always cold."
And Big Mouse pulled the
blanket over his head and
went back to sleep.

Little Mouse got back into his own bed and he lay and listened to the wind huffing and puffing, the branch tap-tapping, and the owl hooting. But sssh! What was that?

"Big Mouse! Big Mouse!" he
called. "I think it's raining inside."
And Little Mouse jumped out of bed
and fetched his red umbrella.

DRIP DRIP DRIP DRIP

Big Mouse got out of bed too. He opened the front door. "Be quiet, wind," he said. "Be quiet, branch. Be quiet, owl." But they took no notice. Then Big Mouse went into the kitchen, turned off the dripping tap and put away the umbrella.

"Can I come into your bed?"
asked Little Mouse.
"No, you're nice and snug in your own bed,"
said Big Mouse, taking him back to the bedroom.

Little Mouse lay and listened
to the wind huffing and
puffing, the branch tap-tapping,
and the owl hooting.
And just as he was beginning
to feel very sleepy indeed,
he heard . . .

"WHEEE,
WHEEE,
WHEEEEE!"

"Big Mouse! Big Mouse!"
he called. "You're snoring."

Wearily Big Mouse got up. He put his ear-muffs on Little Mouse's ears. He put a paper-clip on his own nose, and he went back to bed.

Little Mouse lay and listened to — n o t h i n g !
It was very, very, very quiet. He couldn't hear
the wind huffing or the branch tapping or the owl
hooting or Big Mouse snoring. It was so quiet that
Little Mouse felt he was all alone in the world.

He took off the ear-muffs.
He got out of bed and pulled the paper-clip
off Big Mouse's nose. "Big Mouse! Big Mouse!"
he cried, "I'm lonely!"

Big Mouse flung back
his blanket. "Better come
into my bed," he said.
So Little Mouse hopped
in and his paws
were cold...

and he needed just
a little wriggle before
he fell fast asleep.

Big Mouse lay and listened to the wind huffing and puffing and the branch tapping and the owl hooting and Little Mouse snuffling, and very soon he heard the birds waking up. But neither of them heard the alarm clock…

BECAUSE THEY WERE
BOTH FAST ASLEEP!